# MURDER
# UNLIMITED

Emma Fischel

Illustrated by Ann Johns

Designed by
Paul Greenleaf and Ann Johns

Series Editor: Gaby Waters

# Contents

This is an exciting detective story that you can solve yourself.
Clues and evidence are lurking on almost every page, but stay
alert for red herrings that might put you off the trail.
Vital information may be hidden anywhere, so make sure you read
the text carefully. Look closely at the pictures and study all the
documents and messages.

At various points in the book you will find this symbol $\wp$ . When
you see it, you can refer to the Detective Guide on page 48 for
extra help. The guide will point you in the right direction and give
you handy hints to help work out the mystery. By the end of page 43,
you will have all the information you need to solve the case
before all is finally revealed.

# An Invitation

A letter! Eagerly, Al ripped open the envelope that had just dropped onto the mat. The handwriting seemed vaguely familiar, but whose was it?

Some pieces of paper fell out and she picked them up. It's from Uncle Russ, she thought. But it's not my birthday. Why else would he write to me?

Puzzled, Al began to read. It took quite some time but when she had finished, she went to see her friend Dan. "Take a look at this," she said, handing him the envelope . . .

July 1

Captain Russ I. Rowlocks
Prancing Prawn
Loukaniki Bay
Mythika

My dearest niece Alyssum

How does a week aboard the Prancing Prawn sound? My usual deck crew are away on an Amphibian Recognition course in the first week of August! Would you and a friend stand in for them? The boat has been chartered by Jolyon Scrupulous, some kind of inventor chappie - made himself a small fortune by all accounts. (The booking was strictly secret, but no one seemed interested anyway when I mentioned it in Queezy-Sleezies' cafe a couple of weeks ago.)

I have enclosed my brand new brochure about Prancing Prawn Tours. I'm rather proud of it. (Also enclosed is a photo of the boat.) The people in the brochure photo with me are the other crew members. Max is a dear fellow but temperamental - he's been with me for years. Dida appeared out of the blue about a week ago - an uncanny stroke of luck, almost as if she knew I needed her before I did!

Anyway, I hope you can come. There are daily flights from Delaise airport direct to Loukaniki.

Affectionately, Uncle Russ

## ...G PRAWN TOURS

Hop aboard the Prancing Prawn, the ultimate in comfort and safety! Available for charter from Loukaniki by parties of up to twelve.

- Spacious accommodation, splendid food, sparkling entertainment
- Two sun decks, two lounges, large dining room
- Powerful engine, dinghy with outboard motor, up-to-the-minute radio equipment

*Book early to avoid disappointment! Children under one foot go free! Special rates for the over-80's!*

So sit bac... us do the wo...

With your captain:
- Diamond de'Ath, your friendly hostess. Dida will cater to your every whim. Anything you can think of, she can organize!
- Max Kaloris, wonder chef! Max will tempt your palate daily. Just wait until you taste his pillaka fillets!

...e entertained by performers on the streets of Pathos.

The enchanted world of Mythika and its islands awaits you! Drop anchor in the coastal bays or hop from island to island. The choice is yours!

*A warm and friendly people are waiting to bid you hello!*

3

# On the Waterfront

The morning sun shimmered in a cloudless sky. The heat was already stifling. Al and Dan walked slowly along the waterfront, squinting in the bright early light. In front of them the Fatimian Sea stretched away smooth and still. Hardly a ripple disturbed its surface.

Clutching the photo her uncle had sent, Al looked around for the boat. The tangy smell of salt filled the air. A seagull swooped over their heads. Uttering a mournful cry, it turned and flew out to sea. Soon it was just a tiny speck on the horizon.

A faint breath of wind ruffled the water. Then they saw it – there, bobbing gently at anchor out in the bay, was the Prancing Prawn. Al and Dan stared hard at the boat. This would be their first time at sea, so who could tell what the week might hold in store...

Squalls be a'brewing far out at sea.

Suddenly, Al felt a hand tap her shoulder. She spun around and gasped. Who was this mysterious stranger who stood before her? He began to speak, in low and urgent tones.

When the morning sun blazes from an aquamarine sky, perilous times lie ahead.

Before the tide turns for a fifth time, storm clouds will gather on the horizon.

Mark my words well, young strangers. Danger lies waiting for those who put to sea.

Would he never stop? The stranger stared at them with piercing eyes, blue as the Fatimian Sea, while the prophecies of doom issued from his sun-blistered lips.

Then his face turned pale. He clutched Al's arm and pointed a bony finger at the photo she held in her hand. Once more, he spoke. "There's something bad out there. The birds don't fly near that boat. And the birds always know."

With that, the stranger hurried away, but far down the road he stopped and called back over his shoulder. "Be wary, be watchful – and look out for the fifth turn of the tide." Then he disappeared from view.

For a moment, Al and Dan stood, bemused. But there was no time to wonder. Across the bay came a booming voice. "Ahoy there, landlubbers. Come aboard!"

Waving at them from the deck of the Prancing Prawn was a portly figure dressed in white and blue. And out in the bay a small boat chugged steadily to meet them.

Dida is on her way!

# The Plain Brown Envelope

The Captain gave Al a hearty kiss and Dan a firm handshake as they clambered on deck. "Welcome aboard," he beamed. Meanwhile, Dida bustled busily away.

"We've got a packed week ahead," the Captain continued. "So I've cobbled together a few things you might find it useful to know."

With that, he handed them a plain brown envelope, then left. Al and Dan sat down and began to sift through the contents.

PASSENGERS

Jolyon Scrupulous, millionaire inventor and businessman. Mona Lott, his wife, famous Hollywood actress. Star of box office smash, Eek!. Due to start filming sequel on return from cruise.
Accompanied by Jolyon Junior (JJ), their son.

Cliff Hanger, assistant to Scrupulous for the last five months. Before that was a research scientist studying medical uses for reptile venom.

Rula Margin, nanny to JJ for this trip only. Last-minute replacement for regular nanny who was taken ill.
Oldest of nine children brought up in lighthouse on Hazard Rock. Used to be a nurse.

Dermot Dither, along as my guest. Old school friend. Shared a tambourine in Music and Movement class and been friends ever since. Inclined to be bossy.

CREW

Max Kaloris, chef. Navigator before turned to cookery. Mythikan, but spent much of childhood overseas. Has been jittery and absent-minded lately.

Diamond ('Dida') de'Ath, responsible for passenger care. Seems reluctant to talk about herself, but left last job just over four months ago. Has spent time since on travel.

6

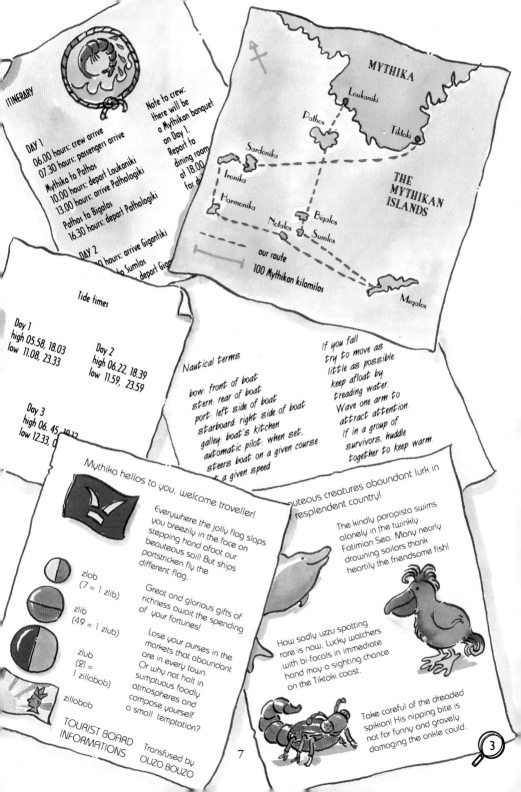

**ITINERARY**

Note to crew:
there will be
a Mythikan banquet
on Day 1.
Report to
dining room
at 18.00
for d...

**DAY 1**
06.00 hours: crew arrive
07.30 hours: passengers arrive
Mythika to Pathos
10.00 hours: depart Loukaniki
13.00 hours: arrive Pathalogiki
Pathos to Bigalos
16.30 hours: depart Pathalogiki

**DAY 2**
...0 hours: arrive Gigantiki
...o Sumlos
...o depart Gig...

**MYTHIKA**

Loukaniki

Pathos

Tiktoki

Sardonika

Ironika

THE
MYTHIKAN
ISLANDS

Harmonika

Notalos

Bigalos

Sumlos

our route
100 Mythikan kilomilos

Megalos

**Tide times**

Day 1
high 05.58, 18.03
low 11.08, 23.33

Day 2
high 06.22, 18.39
low 11.59, 23.59

Day 3
high 06. 45, 19.1...
low 12.33, 0...

**Nautical terms**

bow: front of boat
stern: rear of boat
port: left side of boat
starboard: right side of boat
galley: boat's kitchen
automatic pilot: when set,
steers boat on a given course
...t a given speed

If you fall
try to move as
little as possible.
keep afloat by
treading water.
Wave one arm to
attract attention.
If in a group of
survivors, huddle
together to keep warm.

Mythika hellos to you, welcome traveller!

Everywhere the jolly flag slaps
you breezily in the face on
stepping hand afoot our
beauteous soil! But ships
portstricken fly the
different flag.

Great and glorious gifts of
richness await the spending
of your fortunes!

Lose your purses in the
markets that aboundant
are in every town.
Or why not halt in
sumptuous foodly
atmospheres and
compose yourself
a small temptation?

zlob
(7 = 1 zlib)

zlib
(49 = 1 zlub)

zlub
(21 =
1 zillabob)

zillabob

...uteous creatures aboundant lurk in
resplendent country!

The kindly poropista swims
alonely in the twinkly
Fatimian Sea. Many nearly
drowning sailors thank
heartily the friendsome fish!

How sadly uzzu spotting
rare is now. Lucky watchers
with bi-focals in immediate
hand may a sighting chance
on the Tiktoki coast.

Take careful of the dreaded
spikion! His nipping bite is
not for funny and gravely
damaging the ankle could.

# All Aboard!

The roar of a powerboat approaching made Al and Dan look up from their reading. Then the engine cut out and, through the silence, a voice bellowed out. "Ahoy there, beam us up!"

Jolyon Scrupulous had arrived! He stepped onto the deck, closely followed by his wife and small son. Bringing up the rear was Dermot Dither, struggling with a vast quantity of luggage.

The mega-millionaire and ruthless man of business removed a cigar from between his fat pink lips. "Who's in charge of this floating bathtub?" he asked, as he flicked the soggy stub overboard.

The Captain had just launched into a stiff speech of welcome when a sudden gust of wind took them all by surprise. It blew Dida's hat off, and she leaped to retrieve it. Unfortunately, so did Dither. With a loud crack their heads collided. Irritated by this interruption, the Captain continued. "We leave at ten prompt," he barked. He turned to Al and Dan. "The last provisions will arrive soon. If you need me, I shall be studying my charts." With that, he left.

Jolyon Scrupulous turned to face Dida. "Where's my room?" he demanded, clutching his mobile phone. "I've got calls to make." Dida ushered the new arrivals off to the stairs, leaving Al and Dan alone.

They heard the putt-putt of an ancient engine, followed by a thud as the the Prancing Prawn was rammed in the side by a small boat.

Al and Dan rushed to the rails and looked over the side. The occupants of the boat below seemed to be having some difficulty. A lanky figure dangled half-in and half-out of the water and, wedged awkwardly in the bottom of the boat, was a large pink shape. This must be Cliff Hanger and Rula Margin arriving!

Once on deck the ungainly pair went right away to see Jolyon Scrupulous. Then the stores began to arrive. Two hours later, nearly all the provisions were aboard – but not quite everything...

A couple of smiling characters heaved a huge crate aboard. "We'll secure it nice and tight, then be off," said the one with the hat.

Al rubbed her eyes. Had the one with the hat just winked at the other, or was he squinting in the strong morning light?

At exactly ten the Captain appeared. "Up anchor!" he bellowed, and Al and Dan sprang swiftly into action.

The heavy vibration of the engine throbbed through the boat. Then the Prancing Prawn slewed around and headed slowly out to sea.

But unknown to anyone aboard, someone was watching them leave. Perched high on a hilltop above the town, the mysterious stranger gazed out across the bay.

The eerie cries of the birds that circled around him floated out over the shimmering Fatimian Sea. His piercing blue eyes followed the slow path of the old boat to the distant horizon and, as he watched, was he shaking his head in despair?

9

# Cabin Crew

Al and Dan watched the shoreline gradually fade until it disappeared completely. Then the Prancing Prawn was alone, chugging full steam ahead for the distant island of Pathos. Birds flew high above the sparkling blue sea, but not one flew near the boat.

Once away from the shelter of the land, a stiff breeze whipped salt spray into their faces. Small waves slapped against the hull of the boat. Dan shivered. "Let's find our bunks," he said, and they headed below to look at the boat plan.

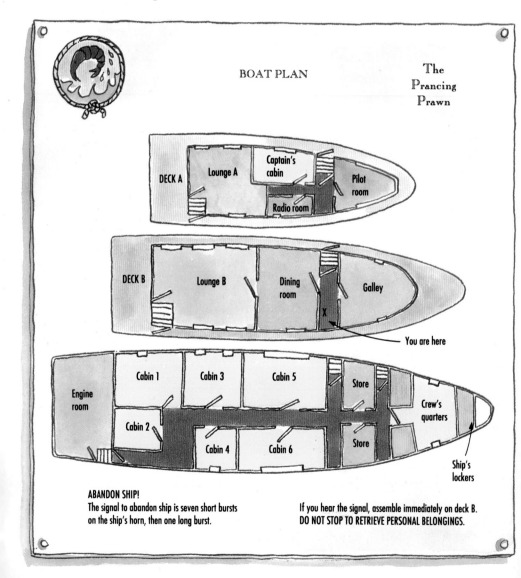

BOAT PLAN

The Prancing Prawn

DECK A — Lounge A — Captain's cabin — Pilot room — Radio room

DECK B — Lounge B — Dining room — Galley — X You are here

Engine room — Cabin 1 — Cabin 3 — Cabin 5 — Store — Crew's quarters — Cabin 2 — Cabin 4 — Cabin 6 — Store — Ship's lockers

**ABANDON SHIP!**
The signal to abandon ship is seven short bursts on the ship's horn, then one long burst.

If you hear the signal, assemble immediately on deck B.
**DO NOT STOP TO RETRIEVE PERSONAL BELONGINGS.**

Dan opened the door to the crew's quarters and inched inside. Al squeezed in behind him. It certainly seemed snug.

Just as they wedged the last of their luggage into the narrow drawers under the bottom bunk, a familiar voice floated in through the open porthole. "Crew on deck!"

The Captain had a long list of chores for the day. "You can start with the portholes," he beamed. "Shouldn't take long once you get into the swing of it."

They quickly realized what the Captain meant. Cleaning some of the portholes proved to be a precarious task...

Soon Dan was dangling from a swinging wooden seat just a few feet above the water. Some job, he thought, as he scrubbed wearily at the glass. This would be his tenth porthole.

He stopped for a moment to rest his aching arms and peered idly into the cabin. Some people do choose to take strange things on a cruise, he mused.

Half an hour later, the final porthole was sparklingly clean. But there was no time to rest. Some energetic deck swabbing lay ahead of them.

Let no one know my job, old man. Makes 'em nervous. Ho ho, see you later.

Al sloshed soapy water over the deck, while Dan scrubbed at the wooden planks. The sounds of conversation drifted down the boat. A booming voice with a hearty laugh seemed to be coming from the radio room.

Ten minutes later, the Captain stamped up to them. He looked red-faced and very angry indeed.

# A Sudden Move

The Captain started to speak in a grumbling voice. "This trip is turning out to be a real headache. First a crate appears out of the blue, cluttering up the deck. No one warned *me*! And the next thing I know, Mr. Extremely Scrupulous tells Dida he wants to move. He claims he doesn't like cabin 6. Ridiculous!"

"So," the Captain continued, with an exasperated sigh, "I want you to move some luggage. I suggest that we move Rula out of cabin 5 to cabin 6, and then our fussy friend into cabin 5."

Leaving the Captain still complaining, Al and Dan headed for cabin 5. Rula's bags lay bulging on the floor. Scooping up one each, Al and Dan staggered to the door. Then Dan stumbled and the bag he was carrying flew out of his hand. It hit the floor. With a loud click, the lid flew up and all the contents spilled out.

**UU Newsletter**

STOP PRESS!!!
*Our breeding site at Happy Days is under threat.*

Donations, urgent stop developers! now!

PPY DAYS HIDEAWAY!
e animals and birds roam free and appy in a natural setting. Sample the delights of a get-away-from-it-all week in one of our camouflaged chalets.

Located just outside the quiet coastal village of Tiktoki, the Happy Days Hideaway will give you a break to remember. "Thank you, Happy Days!" writes RM of Loukaniki. "You made my summer. I'll be back!"

*Our newest little visitor, the uzzu.* Once found all over the globe, this charming little bird is now native only to Mythika. But, thanks to Uzzus Unite, it will soon have a special breeding site in the Happy Days grounds!

△ Over there! Two hikers spot a nesting uzzu.

UZZU SPOTTER'S HANDBOOK

PROTECT OUR UZZUS!

UZZUS UNITE! Member: 27

Al and Dan could hardly believe their eyes. A most peculiar assortment of things littered the floor.

Dan bundled everything back in the case and shut the lid, then Al opened the door. Outside, two people were skulking in the corridor, and they were deep in conversation.

Make no mistake, Rula... going to pay...

Bath every night... five until five-thirty... never varies!

Al and Dan couldn't help overhearing a few snippets of what Cliff and Rula were saying. It seemed to be a very odd discussion indeed.

Then Cliff looked up and saw them. He gave a jump. Nervously, he took out a grubby cotton handkerchief and blew his nose on it noisily.

"Just getting acquainted," tittered Rula. "After all, we are going to be shipmates for quite a while."

Dan was puzzled. From what they had heard it seemed clear that Rula and Cliff were already well acquainted. So why would Rula lie? Before he could wonder any more, the sound of a high-pitched, angry voice drifted out into the corridor. It was coming from inside cabin 6.

This is the last straw. This time you've gone too far!

About time!

How nice!

Outside cabin 6, Al hesitated, then she lifted her hand and rapped on the door. Nervously, she pushed it open. Not everyone inside the cabin seemed entirely happy. "Our luggage is on the bed over there," snapped Jolyon Scrupulous. "Move it now!"

Al and Dan hurried across the room. All of a sudden, there was a furious noise from outside – the noise of feet pounding along the corridor at great speed. Then the cabin door burst open.

Everyone inside the room recoiled in horror. In front of them was a wild-eyed figure, maddened with rage. And in his hand he brandished a very sharp bread knife...

# The Missing Melons

Someone aboard this boat is a thief!

T his must be Max Kaloris! Puce with rage, he glared around cabin 6. "My entire stock of melons – stolen!" he bellowed, slicing the bread knife through the air. Then he turned to Jolyon Scrupulous. "And by one of your party!" he hissed.

"They were there at ten, ripened to perfection," elaborated the Mythikan master chef. "But by noon, there they were, gone! Wait until I find the culprit...!" With that, he flounced out of the room and slammed the door. A folded piece of paper fluttered to the floor behind him.

For a moment everyone stood stunned. Then Al heaved a couple of suitcases off the bed. "Let's go," she said to Dan, picking up the piece of paper by the door on her way out.

At last the move was completed. Leaving the new occupants of cabins 5 and 6 to settle in, Al and Dan went up on deck.

Look. Melon seeds!

They stared down at their feet. A sticky trail of melon juice, not yet dried by the sun, dribbled along deck A. Every so often, clumps of seeds lay splattered on the varnished wooden planks. Then the trail stopped. But behind the boat, a line of melon rinds bobbed about in the choppy wake left by the Prancing Prawn.

"Who on earth would steal the melons?" asked Al, confused. Before Dan could reply a deafening crash echoed around the boat, followed by a muffled scream and strange thumping, groaning noises...

14

# A Narrow Escape

Al and Dan pounded down the stairs. The sound of running feet came from all directions. It seemed everyone had heard the noise. Dither overtook them in the corridor. "I'll deal with this. Stand back," he ordered, flinging open the door to cabin 6.

Just then, the ship's horn sounded. With a shudder, the engine began to slow down. They were arriving at Pathos.

# Surprises on Shore

The Prancing Prawn chugged into the port. Dither stayed below to comfort a shaken Rula, while everyone else rushed on deck. It was market day and the busy waterfront was bustling with life.

Clutching a long shopping list, Al and Dan hurried ashore and into the thick of the market. The main street was packed with stalls groaning under the weight of piles of exotic food.

At two o'clock, hot, weary and hungry, they bought a snack. Al spent two zlob on a slice of Pathosian snibblebite, while Dan chose a juicy malingo fruit. Outside the door of the Mythikan National Bank they started to eat, then suddenly they heard a great commotion.

Al and Dan watched in amazement as a figure hurtled out of the bank door, propelled by the heavy hand of a burly security guard. It was Cliff! He lay on the dusty street, shouting.

The security guard remained unmoved. "Boss's new rule. No credit and no time to pay," she growled.

Cliff picked himself up. He didn't notice Al or Dan. "I'll get the money, you'll see," he muttered, turning to go. "I'll just have to act faster than planned."

16

What was all that about? Confused, Al and Dan made their way to Ouzo the Outfitters. They each had four zlub to spend on a Mythikan national costume for the evening's banquet.

It was difficult to concentrate on the suggestions of the helpful shop assistant. A hissing voice was filtering through the patterned curtain of the changing room. And from what they could hear, the owner of the voice sounded furious about something.

At last the bitter outburst came to a halt and, with a swish of the curtain, who should come out but Mona! Tight-lipped, she swirled out of the shop in a cloud of strong perfume.

After that, Al and Dan were hardly aware of what outfits they chose. They left the shop with two brightly wrapped bundles.

They made their way back to the Prancing Prawn. By four-thirty, the boat was on its way to Bigalos and, with some relief, Al and Dan headed below deck to their cabin.

"What a peculiar day!" said Dan, collapsing in an exhausted heap on the bottom bunk.

"Mmm," agreed Al with a groan. "And it's not over yet." She shifted uncomfortably on the hard bunk. Something rustled in her back pocket and she jumped up. Of course! She had forgotten all about the piece of paper Max had dropped earlier.

She fished it out of her pocket, unfolded it and tried to smooth out the crumples. It was a magazine article. Something in it caught her eye...

17

# STAR GAZING

**Juster Snoop profiles Jolyon Scrupulous, the man with the millions!**

"Unpopular – me? Of course! I've never cared about being liked. That's why I'm rich!" Jolyon Scrupulous, millionaire inventor now turned businessman, was speaking by the pool of his luxury villa in Tiktoki. "I've built my fortune by inventing useless things," he chortled. "Then I persuade people that they need them!"

We were interrupted by shouts from behind the high-security gates. Protesters from a local nature sanctuary were out in force. Jolyon plans to build a leisure centre that will cut through the sanctuary and halt proposals for an uzzu haven. After a small scuffle the protesters were ejected.

> **"I've never cared about being liked. That's why I'm rich!"**

Unperturbed, Jolyon continued our interview. "In my position you can't afford to mind what people think of you," he said. But did he gaze wistfully for a moment at his little son splashing in the pool?

## Business buying

Over the last three years, Jolyon's inventions have made him millions. Now he is expanding his horizons. In a shock move nearly five months ago, he bought up the Tuffaware All-Weather Anorak chain. That was swiftly followed by the acquisition of the Mythikan National Bank. Jolyon's methods have caused strong murmurs of disapproval in the business community. He plans a change in loan policy at Mythikan National that will leave thousands of customers losers, leading some to call him the most ruthless business brain of the decade.

▼ Family man Jolyon likes nothing better than the rare opportunity to relax at home.

▲ Jolyon stays in shape with a brisk swim each morning – in between business deals!

▲ Jolyon and his tragic former partner on the way to discuss the Tuffaware take-over bid.

## Surprise marriage

After a whirlwind courtship two years ago, Jolyon married Hollywood film star Mona Lott. "He just swept me off my feet," said Mona after the secret wedding in Las Tingbliss.

Friends of the star had long expected that she would marry her producer Sven Gayley, who some credit with her success. Their stormy relationship and massive public arguments had led many to suspect a romance between the pair but, instead, they settled recently for a ten-year contract.

## Tragic accident

"It was the biggest shock of my life!" said Jolyon, talking about the recent sad disappearance of his business partner. Best known as the former child-star impressionist Teeny Dimple, his partner disappeared in mysterious circumstances in March, missing presumed drowned.

> **"It was the biggest shock of my life!"**

One source believes Jolyon's partner was very disturbed by the move into take-overs, and may even have been collecting information about fraudulent business deals.

***Scoop!*** We can exclusively reveal that Mona and Jolyon have chartered a Loukanikian cruiser in August. Look out Mythikans!

## Rags to riches

The Scrupulous story began when the poor boy from Lessenless County gained an early scholarship to Ablution College, famous throughout the world for its academic excellence. There his brilliant mind

> **"Scrupulous used to pick on me!"**

shone through, although he was not popular and gained a reputation as something of a bully.

One old classmate claims he lived in daily fear: "Scrupulous used to pick on me and pinch my pastry cutter, just because I liked to spend weekends sticking recipes in my scrapbook."

## Career changes

On leaving school, Jolyon dabbled in many things. As a student biochemist he spent a year in isolated and treacherous conditions up the Intrepid river studying the plant and animal life. Then he turned to banking, followed by a spell on an oil tanker. After that came SLIME, and the foundation of the whole Scrupulous empire . . .

▲ A rare photo of Jolyon the schoolboy, having fun with his classmates.

◀ As a student, living rough up the wild Intrepid river.

## SLIME

SLIME was the brainchild of Jolyon Scrupulous and his former business partner. Together they created a dynamic new computer program that rocked the world and led them to fame and fortune. Launched onto the market with a massive billboard campaign reproduced below, the eager public couldn't buy it fast enough. People queued in the streets to get their hands on it. Shops sold out as fast as new stocks arrived. Copies were exchanging hands for fantastic sums. Then the government stepped in and the product was banned. But it had already made Jolyon millions.

---

# *SLIME*

**Supersonic Lies Incorporating Mega Excuses**

Lie your way out of any tricky situation!

**Haven't done your homework?
Late for work again?
Forgot to go to your wedding?
Pan-fried your best friend?**

*Just tap in your problem,
**SLIME** will give you the solution!
Excuses for every occasion!*

★ *SLIME changed my life!*
Miss O Dear, Pankhurst Prison

★ *Brilliant! I use it every day!*
Freckles, Swotville

★ *Thank you, SLIME!*
Teacher, Truanting College

# Chef's Special

With a loud dong, the ship's clock struck six. "Quick!" said Dan, putting down the magazine article. "The Mythikan banquet!" Then he shot off in the direction of the stairs.

Strange smells were wafting out of the galley as they reached the dining room. Inside, Dida was tapping her foot impatiently.

What a meal! Course followed course.

I eat like a bird.

More bread.

Until...

GREED CONQUERS ALL

But there was a snag.

Mine's not big enough!

And a solution.

Swap!

Every bite seemed better than the last. Then there was a loud crash.

Splurg!

Wheeeoooop!

Dither went to the rescue.

Oooooggh!

Easy now!

He sniffed the remains, then spoke.

Tedium hypochondriade, fast-acting and fatal in large doses. This woman has been poisoned. It is a miracle she is still alive!

21

13

# Dither Takes Charge

A stunned silence greeted Dither's statement. Jolyon Scrupulous was the first to recover. "Nonsense," he said impatiently. "A case of mild food poisoning, that's all. Anyway, who are you to take charge?" Dither glared, then fumbled around in his pocket...

Dermot Dither
Special Agent

Dither
of the Yard!

Dither flourished his ID card importantly. "I came here in a civilian capacity," he said. "But now it seems my professional skills are needed."

Shrewdly, he scrutinized the group in front of him. "We appear to have a cold-blooded attempt at poisoning. And is it coincidence that a deadly snake was on the loose earlier? I think not!"

The Captain was in some distress. "I can't believe this could happen," he muttered. "I run a tight ship. What should I do?"

"Rowlocks," said Dither, patting his old friend kindly on the shoulder. "I suggest you start by fetching Kaloris. There are a few questions he needs to answer."

It is a crime to do this to my baked balikis! And you accuse me – me! I loved that dish!

Three minutes later Max appeared. He seemed upset. Dither spoke with authority. "Calm down," he ordered. "No one is accusing you of anything – yet."

"It is likely that the poison was added in the galley," Dither continued. "But who had the opportunity? Max, of course, but did he leave the galley at any point, I wonder? Anyone else could have done it then."

"At six o'clock I went to talk to the Captain," said Max, sniffling. "I had just made the balikis. I left them on a tray, ready for baking later. It was six thirty-five when I returned."

Dither's eyes moved slowly over face after face. "In that case, I must ask each of you to account for your movements between six o'clock and the evening meal," he said solemnly.

There was a buzz of outrage. Then the Captain spoke. "Surely you can't mean to include Mona or Rula," he objected gallantly. "They were the victims!"

"Were they? Victims of what? After all, neither attempt actually worked," said Dither. "No, until we know what we are dealing with – and why – no one can be excluded." Before anyone could raise more objections, he continued. "Something strange is going on aboard this boat. We need to find out what before anything worse happens!"

Reluctantly, one by one they disclosed their whereabouts. Then again Dither spoke, in a voice loaded with warning. "Ladies and gentlemen, I suggest we take the quickest possible route to land. Until then, I urge you all to tread very carefully indeed. Exercise the utmost caution. Go to your cabins and lock the doors. Speak to no one until we arrive in port, or who can tell who might be the next victim!"

# What Next?

There was an uneasy silence after Dither's words. Then the Captain spoke. "We'll turn back to Pathos. With the wind and tide against us, I estimate it will take seven hours. But going on to Bigalos would take much longer." Hurriedly, he left.

Soon the frightened group made their way to the cabin deck. Doors slammed and keys turned, then Dither stationed himself on guard.

Inside the crew's quarters, Al got out her brand-new notepad and pen set. She began to write...

ATTEMPT 1 - RULA

Time: 12.30.
Place: Cabin 6
Method: A bucket over her head while a snake was on the loose in her cabin.

Who would have a bucket - or a snake?

Does anyone know about snakes (apart from Dither)?

Was anyone acting suspiciously?

Can we rule out Jolyon and Mona? (We were with them almost until we heard the scream.)

ATTEMPT 2 - MONA

Time: 20.10
Place: Dining room
Method: Poison in the baked baliki.
She only had a few mouthfuls of baliki - someone greedier would have been killed.

When was the baliki poisoned?
Who was sitting where at the table?
Is it important?
Can we believe what everyone said?
Is anyone lying?
Does anyone (apart from Dither) know about snakes?

Things we need to find out

1) Why would anyone want to murder both Rula and Mona?
2) Could the attacks be random? No - that's silly.
3) Is there anything that links the two attempts - anything similar about them?

Things that don't make sense

1) Who took the melons?
2) Why was Max carrying the magazine article around? (Does he usually read The Weekly Twitter?)
3) Why are Cliff and Rula pretending not to know each other? What was that conversation we overheard on the cabin deck all about?

RULA

Victim. Why?
What about her luggage?
Has been to Happy Days
Hideaway in Tiktoki. Is
this important?

MONA

Victim. Why?
What about her conversation
in Ouzo the Outfitters? Who
was she speaking to?
Suspiciously unable to
remember what she was
doing between six and the
meal. Unable or unwilling?

MAX

Easy for him to poison the
baliki – but for what
motive? Too obvious?

UNCLE RUSS AND DITHER

Above suspicion?

What else do we know about anyone?
Is there anything we have overlooked?

CLIFF

Was he in his cabin when
he said he was?
What about that strange
scene outside the
Mythikan National Bank?

DIDA

Was she in the dining
room all the time
between six and the
meal? Would we have
noticed if she had
left (we were very
busy)?

SEND MUM
POSTCARD

JOLYON SCRUPULOUS

Why did he change cabins?
Should we read the
magazine article again?

Buy Spiodge a present

"That wasn't much help," sighed
Al as she put the lid back on the pen.

Dan drummed his heels nervously on the floor. Someone aboard was
the villainous would-be killer. But who? And would they get safely to port
before he or she struck again?

Al yawned. "I can't think any more," she said. "Let's set the alarm for
four. We should be nearly at Pathos by then." But little did she know,
things weren't going to go quite according to plan...

25

# Sabotage!

Rrrring! It was four o'clock. Blearily, Al and Dan stumbled out onto the chilly deck. Pale fingers of light were just streaking the sky. Surely there should be some sign of Pathos by now? But all they could see was choppy grey sea in all directions.

Oooourrrgh!

"What was that noise?" said Al suddenly. "I think it came from one of the cabins!" They rushed below decks and found Dither inching the engine room door open. Strange moaning sounds were coming from inside. "Leave this to me," hissed Dither.

"Captain Rowlocks!"
"My dear chap!"
"What happened, Uncle Russ?"

Shocked, they all spoke at once. At the foot of the stairs, the Captain lay slumped. "I went to turn the boat around," he groaned. "But everything was jammed. Calamity! I hurried down here to sort things out..."

The light wouldn't work.

Then I heard a noise.

CRRRRK!

Fearlessly, I called out.

H-h-halloooo?

Suddenly I saw something. I spun around.

Who's there?

I saw the frozen chicken too late!

"I must have been knocked out cold," concluded the Captain. "The next thing I knew, I was lying where you found me."

"Impossible!" blustered Dither. "Why, I was on watch the whole time. Who could have passed me?"

"No idea," said the Captain, struggling to stand up. He blew his nose loudly. "First a roving reptile, then poison, now sabotage! Never, in all my years at sea – "

"Let's radio for help," interrupted Dither decisively. Al, Dan and the Captain followed him along the corridor. There was no noise from any of the cabins. Everyone seemed to be sleeping very soundly.

Inside the radio room, a shock lay in store...

"Things are looking grim," said Dither gravely. He clutched onto a table as he spoke. The old boat was beginning to roll more and more in the increasing swell. Outside, storm clouds were gathering in a darkening sky. "We can't change course," he continued. "We can't change speed, and we can't radio for help!"

The Captain had been doing some calculations. He spoke heavily. "It appears that we are locked on course for Megalos. And that's twenty-four hours away!"

# Man Overboard

Twenty-four hours! This was a new and dangerous development. The only course of safety now was to stick together. On Dither's orders, Al and Dan hurried to wake everyone and bring them to lounge B.

"First murder, now sabotage. What on – oof!" said Al, cannoning into Dan. He had stopped abruptly, halfway down the stairs.

"Did you hear something?" he asked, starting to run. "Like a faint cry?"

"Not again!" said Al. She struggled to keep up as she pounded along in his footsteps.

"It's coming from over the side!" said Dan, racing along deck B.

"Impossible!" said Al in disbelief.

Then she saw the mega-magnate – and what a sight he made. Pink-faced and grunting, he dangled from the flagpole, saved from a watery grave only by the grip of his fingers.

"Help me!" he bellowed at the top of his voice as he bounced over the choppy wave tops. The flimsy wooden flagpole swayed and bent from side to side. It looked as if it might break at any moment.

"Man overboard!" shouted Al efficiently. Soon, her shouts brought people rushing out on deck.

"Hold on!" commanded Dither, taking charge. He leaped onto the guard rails. Then the tricky process of hauling the mighty mogul back on deck began. It proved to be no easy task...

At last the spluttering Scrupulous was safely hauled aboard. He collapsed on the deck, outraged. "Just what kind of boat is this?" he roared. "I come aboard expecting a nice relaxing break and what happens? – murder and mayhem, that's what!"

Then, swaddled in warm, dry blankets and clutching a large medicinal glass of Mythikan bouzo, Jolyon Scrupulous calmed down enough to tell his story. "I was out for an early morning stroll, mulling over an idea for a new kind of slug collar," he said, with a big barking cough. "I was leaning over the back of the boat watching the water."

"The next thing I knew – bam! – I felt a great big shove in the back. I lost my balance and over I went!" he concluded indignantly.

It's only by a stroke of luck I'm still here to tell the tale!

But someone on deck had no need to listen to Jolyon's story. Someone knew what had happened. Someone knew what the mega-millionaire was going to say before he spoke. But who? Who was the villainous perpetrator of the fiendish attempt on Jolyon's life?

# Speedy Exits

Drops of rain began to spatter the deck as Jolyon finished his tale. By now, the boat was heaving in and out of the increasing swell. Dither hurried everyone into lounge B. He spoke solemnly. "We are in a desperate predicament!" To gasps of shock and horror, Dither spelled out the damage to the radio and engine.

"Murder unlimited!" Dither continued gravely. "That is what we are dealing with. We must assume there have been at least three attempts – and some very narrow escapes." Swaying with the motion of the boat, he turned to face Jolyon Scrupulous. "Indeed, it is pure chance our friend is here at all!"

"Oh yes," continued Dither. "There is a villain in our midst. And he or she may strike again. But at who? If only we could find some connection between all these events. Alas, there is none!"

"At the heart of the matter lies motive," pronounced Dither, staggering as the boat rolled first one way then the other. "And there is our problem," he said solemnly. "Find a motive, find a victim, find an opportunity – and, my friends, you find a murderer!"

Dither seemed to be losing his audience. The Captain was the first to bolt – but not the last. In ones and twos they tottered away...

...until only Al, Dan and Dither were left.

Dither turned to Al and Dan. "Now then, you two," he said bossily, with a twirl of his moustache. "I suggest you – "

Al and Dan waited patiently for him to continue. "Hrrrmph," he said, after a pause. Then, faintly, "Must go and er, splurrrg." And with that, he ran out of the room...

How do you feel?

Fine! But what do we do now?

Judging by the green faces of their departing companions, Al and Dan were safe enough from any more villainy for the moment. Heads whirling, they tried to make sense of things.

"So, the first victim was Rula," said Al. "Then there was Mona. Last of all, Jolyon Scrupulous was pushed overboard. But why? What reason would anyone have?"

Dan was silent. Something Dither had said earlier was nagging away at the back of his mind. Something about Mona and the poison. Or was it about Rula and the snake? If only he could remember. He was sure it held a vital clue to the would-be murderer's identity.

"And what about the engine?" continued Al. "Who would know how to sabotage that? Then there's the mystery of the Captain's injury and the smashed radio. Dither says no one left any of the cabins!"

"What a puzzle," said Dan. "The only connection appears to be that there is no connection. But there must be one!" He paused, despairing. "The more we think, the more confused it gets. Let's start again. First, Rula was nearly murdered in her cabin."

"What did you say?" said Al.

Dan sighed. "I said, first Rula was nearly murdered in her – "

"But it wasn't her cabin," said Al. "Not to start with! Then Mona. Whose food did she eat? And the third attempt..."

"...was the right person!" finished Dan triumphantly.

He must be warned!

Let's hope it's not too late.

31

# Inside Cabin 5

Al and Dan staggered down to the cabin deck. It was hard to keep upright as the old boat battled through the heavy seas. They went straight in to cabin 5. This was no time to knock and wait.

It took a moment to attract the attention of the grumpy magnate. He turned around, frowning. Falteringly, Al and Dan explained their conclusions. His frown grew bigger and bigger.

"Preposterous!" said Jolyon Scrupulous. "I have enemies, of course. What person of power doesn't? And there are secrets here that could be worth a fortune to my rivals." The tycoon proudly waved a hand at a pile of neatly stacked boxes. "But murder? Who would dare?"

Suddenly, the boat lurched down into the trough of a particularly large wave. The pile of boxes started to wobble...

Once all the boxes were back in place, Jolyon Scrupulous knotted a length of strong cord tightly around them. Al and Dan tried once again to make him understand his life might be in danger. But it was useless. The mega-millionaire refused to listen.

"Nonsense," he snorted. "I, Jolyon Scrupulous, have the world at my fingertips. In any city in the world, all it takes is a phone call – and in ten minutes I can do anything! And now you tell me that some second-rate assassin is after me. Me! I think not!"

At that moment, there was a scuffling noise from the corridor. Was someone outside the door, listening to their conversation?

"A threat from the murderer!" gasped Al. She turned to Jolyon Scrupulous. His face had gone very pale. He seemed in a severe state of shock. For once, he appeared to have nothing to say.

Dan was puzzled. Somehow, it just didn't seem to fit. Would the ruthless villain who had carried out the vicious string of crimes really have written that petulant note?

Mona broke the silence. "One thing is certain, whoever tried to push you overboard must be watching your every movement," she began. "After all, it's very rare for you to get up so early. But who can it be? It must be one of your many enemies who is behind all these attempts on your life!"

"Ridiculous!" said Jolyon Scrupulous. "The idea of someone aboard trying to kill me! And do you think I would not recognize one of my enemies?"

# Heading for Trouble

Clutching a bottle of Wundaworka, Al and Dan lurched out of cabin 5. They knocked on the door opposite. The boat was rolling and pitching heavily from side to side. How much worse could things get?

Rula greeted Al and Dan in a quavering and feeble voice. She gave up her struggle to read. Gratefully, she swallowed a dose of Wundaworka. Almost immediately, a tinge of pink returned to her cheeks.

"That's better," she said. "I'm trying hard to study for the second year of my soothsaying course. It starts in only two weeks."

The next stop was Cliff's cabin. He was just finishing a letter when they went in. He looked ill – and agitated.

Soon the Wundaworka took its effect on him. "If only everything was so easily cured," he said with a trace of bitterness. It was almost as if he was talking to himself.

Al and Dan left Cliff mumbling in his cabin. He seemed eager for them to go. On unsteady feet, they headed for Dida's cabin and rapped on the door.

Had she heard them knock? Swaying, Al and Dan waited – and waited. It seemed to be a long time before she answered.

At last Dida eased the door open a fraction. She looked flustered. Her hair was dishevelled. She didn't let them in, but stood clutching onto the door while she took the medicine.

"There's a storm ahead," said Al.

"You may be right," muttered Dida. "I fear you may be right."

There was no one in either of the other cabins. Clinging onto the handrails, Al and Dan went up the stairs. By now the wind was howling around the boat. Huge thunderclouds blocked out the sun. It was nearly midday, but so dark it could have been the middle of the night.

Al and Dan knocked at the door to the Captain's cabin. Max opened it. "They're both in pretty bad shape," he warned, letting them in.

Dan moved over to the two sickly chums. He got out the Wundaworka, then blinked. It was dark, but had a shadowy figure, or even two, just passed the window?

Dither recovered quickly. "Now, where was I," he said. "Who could the villain be?" He straightened his bow tie. "They say it's the quiet ones you should watch," he mused. "And, of course, often it's the least likely person – "

But the Captain had been listening to none of this. He had been studying the towering waves through the window. Now he spoke.

Suddenly, Al and Dan remembered the mysterious stranger on the shores of Loukaniki bay. What was it he had said about the tide?

Back in their cabin, Al made some quick calculations. She looked at Dan. "This will be the fifth turn of the tide," she said uneasily.

Dong! The ship's clock struck twelve. A huge streak of lightning lit up the sky, then a giant clap of thunder shook the boat...

# The Storm

Would the storm never end? The Prancing Prawn floundered helplessly in the angry seas. Hour after hour, the gallant old boat was tossed and thrown around by the giant waves. The wind roared, the waves raged, and icy spray smacked down on the drenched and salty deck. All the passengers could do was cower in their cabins.

At last the storm began to ease. Al and Dan staggered out on deck. Then things happened thick and fast...

The door would hardly open in the wind.

There had been a few casualties.

Suddenly...

Look!

Al and Dan watched the Potted Shrimp drift away.

The dinghy!

Then the clouds burst open.

Al and Dan ran for shelter.

Did they hear a faint cry, whipped away by the wind?

Had that been the sound of running feet?

Inside, Al's foot touched something soft and squishy. . .

# Under the Blankets

Al and Dan gaped down. A sodden bundle of old blankets at their feet started to move – and speak...

Then two dripping figures emerged, whimpering, from the pile of damp blankets. "Who-who are you?" gasped Dan. Before the pitiful pair could answer, the Captain and Dither arrived. Between them, they had plenty of questions for the trembling twosome.

The soggy stowaways seemed unable to say a word.

"Clap 'em in irons!" roared the Captain.

"Calm yourself, Russ, old boy," commanded Dither. "Now then," he said, to the dripping duo. "Let's start again. Who are you and what are you doing on this ship?"

"W-we are the Bungla brothers," said the one with the hat. "I'm Bala, this is Klava. We got a phone call yesterday from someone aboard this boat. We were hired to murder Jolyon Scrupulous!"

"But no one mentioned hurricanes," added the other Bungla bitterly.

"And might this be your calling card?" asked Dither sternly. He pulled a soggy piece of cardboard out of Bala Bungla's pocket and held it out for everyone to read.

DOUBLE TROUBLE

We despatch anything!

Free estimates. No job too small. Contact us at Queezy-Sleezies.

Everyone read the words in silence. Then Dither spoke. "So, who hired you? When? And why?"

The boss has had a call. The contract is out on Scrupulous! Here's what you do.

Once again, it was Bala who answered. "It all started at nine o'clock yesterday morning. We were sitting in Queezy-Sleezies, enjoying a malingo sling each and playing chek-choki..."

"The mystery caller gave us some instructions. When the crate arrived we took it to the boat, strapped it down, and left," continued Bala. "Afterwards, we sneaked back on board by climbing up the anchor chain. We hid in the crate. There was a lot of equipment inside – "

"The snake gave us a bit of a surprise," added Klava.

Once the Bungla brothers had started, they seemed only too eager to reveal everything they knew...

We never saw who hired us, just heard his voice. He sounded strange.

It was a woman.

A man. Anyway, we met this *person* twice on board. He – or she – insisted we wore blindfolds. We met first to set up the bucket and snake plan.

How could we know Scrupulous would swap cabins? We're assassins, not mind-readers!

The second meeting was at six-fifteen that evening. After that we poisoned the baliki.

We didn't expect him to exchange plates like that!

The mystery person told us how to sabotage the engine and radio. Then the Captain appeared. Disaster!

Lucky I had stolen the frozen chicken from the galley!

"And what about the anonymous letter?" asked Dither when the Bunglas came to the end of their list of dastardly actions. "And the other attempt on Jolyon Scrupulous?"

"What?" exclaimed Bala and Klava together. "We never – "

Just then Max burst in. "Something terrible has happened!" he gasped.

28

# Some Interesting Reading

Max struggled to speak. "It's Dida," he sobbed. "She's nowhere to be found. She must have fallen overboard!"

Dither was quick to react. "Fallen... or pushed? Russ, gather everyone into the lounge. I'm going to search the boat for clues!"

While Dither poked and prodded his way around the cabins, Al and Dan told him everything they had discovered since they came aboard. "Hmmm. Interesting," said Dither, with a smile and a twirl of his moustache. "But I think you can leave the detective work to me."

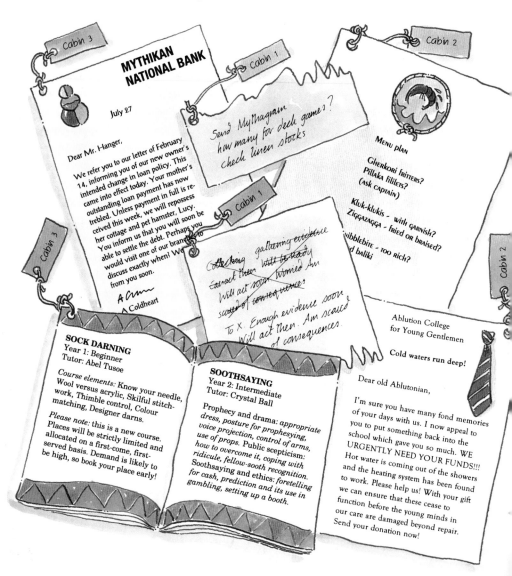

At last, every room had been searched. Al and Dan laid all the exhibits out on the dining room table. "Right," said Dither importantly. "Somewhere in here I'll find a clue to the mystery villain – the unsuccessful assassin who succeeds only in killing the wrong person!"

Dan thought about what Dither had just said. He was getting a glimmer of an idea. Maybe things were not quite what they seemed. And the bits of paper in front of them made some very interesting reading indeed. Had they been on the wrong track all along?

Cabin 6

Ideas • Inventions • Innovations

**STREETS AHEAD**

July 27

Dear Ms. M,

We were most interested to hear your proposition. Naturally we would be prepared to pay the highest rates to you and your associate for information about competitive products. Perhaps we ...uld talk again?

Cabin 5

Cabin 5

**SHARP AND BENT LAWYERS**

Your trouble is our business!

August 1

My dear sister

I have done as you suggested and have found a firm of lawyers. On my return we will set the wheels in motion ...ns get out I can't go on...

Cabin 5

July 28

Dear Mr. Scrupulous

It is our intention to visit your premises on August 13. We will require access to all your files and all personnel. We shall expect confirmation of this appointment from you within the next week.

Think we'll be OK. Anyway there is no one to testify against us - is there?

Xavier Niceday
Fraud Squad

**MYTHAGRAM**

To Jolyon Scrupulous. July 29

'TD' ON YOUR TRAIL.
WATCH YOUR BACK.

...sses

Mona

Cabin 6

Rula,

We were delighted to hear of your forthcoming donation to the Happy Days Uzzu Haven. If you agree, we would like to erect a statue in a corner of the sanctuary in thanks to our greatest benefactor! With eager anticipation.

Lily Pond

# Accusations Fly

Dither muttered and sucked in his cheeks as he read. At last he looked up. "Right. Some people have a lot of explaining to do," he said, heading for the lounge.

Al and Dan followed him. Things had become much clearer to both of them. It seemed that, all along, they had been busy thinking exactly the way the villain wanted – but no longer...

Dither stomped up to the shocked group huddled around the table. "A strange and brutal drama has unfolded before us," he began. "First, we have the Bungla brothers. A nasty pair of hired thugs, but small fry – the minor players. What we are after is the lead! Who is the fiend who hired the duo and then brutally took matters into his or her own hands? This villain must be found!"

"To that end we searched the cabins," Dither continued. "It proved most revealing. Coupled with what my young friends here have discovered, we seem to have some very guilty people in this room indeed."

"You see, my friends, we know everything," Dither continued. "What do you have to say for yourselves?" For a moment the wretched villains sat stunned, then they spoke anxiously in their defence.

> He wouldn't remember Blubberface Kaloris. But I remembered him. Years at school he made my life a misery. When he chartered the boat I planned to get even.

> We met at evening class. We discovered our common enemy and started planning. First Cliff got himself the job with Scrupulous. We saw our chance when the nanny's job came up.

> We pretended not to know each other. That way no one would link us once the prototypes were sold.

> You're wrong. That letter, those phone calls, they were about Sven Gayley, my producer. I'm trying to break my contract. I love my husband!

"It was wrong – but I only wanted to frighten him," said Max. "My uzzus need a sanctuary. But murder – never!" said Rula. "I only wanted to steal for mummy's sake," said Cliff.

The suspects all spoke at once. Dither was confused. "You all have reason to wish Jolyon Scrupulous harm," he said plaintively. "But reason enough to plot murder?" He rubbed his head. "Let me collect my thoughts. First, there was the snake, then the poison. Both were cases of bad planning, almost bound to lead to failure. This was the work of a second-rate villain – "

Al interrupted. "You're wrong. Someone is being very clever indeed – "

Dither glared at her and continued. "Next, the sabotage of the engine and the injury to our poor captain. Then the villain takes over from the Bunglas. And the sad result is, at the second attempt, a murder. Someone died – but the wrong someone! Although how anyone could mistake Dida for Jolyon Scrupulous, even in a torrential storm, is beyond me!"

32

"So there you have it," Dither concluded. "Someone in this room is lying, but who? Which one of you is the ruthless killer?"

Dan took a deep breath, then spoke. "All the pieces are in place," he said. "We know who did it, and why!"

---

**STOP. DON'T TURN THE PAGE YET.** You now have all the information you need to solve the string of contemptible crimes. Can you reveal the identity of the dastardly villain?

# All is Revealed

To begin with, nothing made sense.

Astonished, everyone stared at Al and Dan. Then Dither spoke. "How can you possibly know the identity of the killer?" he said. "We've had exactly the same information!"

"I'd like to hear what they have to say," interrupted Jolyon Scrupulous with a toothy smile. "It might be interesting."

Nervously, Al began. "At first everything seemed unconnected – but there *had* to be a link somewhere. The first task was to find it. After the attempt on Jolyon Scrupulous it seemed clear that he was the target. It was only by pure chance the first two attempts had failed."

"Then we started to have doubts," continued Dan. "There seemed to be no one aboard with a true motive for murder. And there was something odd about the murder attempts. Had they really been serious? It seemed almost as if the villain wanted to fail. But what possible reason could he or she have? It was Dither himself who gave us the clue..."

... the unsuccessful assassin who succeeds only in killing the wrong person!

"But was it the wrong person?" said Al. "Look at the facts alone. Dida was pushed overboard. Just suppose that wasn't a mistake. If we stop assuming the target was Jolyon Scrupulous and assume instead that it was Dida, the attempt becomes successful!"

"Maybe all the time we were thinking along the wrong lines," said Dan. "And suppose that was because, for some reason, the murderer had made us do that!"

"Once again," continued Al, "It was thinking back to something Dither had said earlier that helped us slot things into place..."

... until we know what we are dealing with – and why – no one can be excluded.

"At the time, Dither meant that Mona and Rula could not be excluded from suspicion because they were victims," said Dan. "Yet later we all left one person off the suspect list, purely because he appeared to be the intended victim!"

"Don't you see?" said Al. "The attempts on Jolyon Scrupulous were a sham. They were meant to disguise the real murder – of Dida!"

"And only one person on this boat would have the deviousness to hatch such a fiendish plot!" said Dan.

44

"But why? We were stumped for a motive," said Dan. He tried to ignore the muttered comments around him, and continued. "Then we remembered the magazine article. Was it possible his former business partner, the holder of murky secrets about his shady dealings, had suddenly reappeared to tell all? If so, this could mean ruin!"

Al pointed accusingly at Jolyon Scrupulous. "You recognized Dida as your old partner and leaped into action! You set yourself up as the apparent target. Who would suspect you then? With your connections it wasn't difficult to do. A few phone calls secured the crate, the snake, the poison, the Bunglas. And just to make quite sure Dida didn't contact anyone, some sabotage – "

"Very clever," snarled the villain. "But where's your proof?"

"The Bunglas said the person who hired them had a strange voice," said Dan. "Among your prototypes is a voice transformer. You have the engine manual in your cabin. And I'm sure if we searched carefully, we'd find some trace of the sleeping drug you used on Mona when you went to meet the Bunglas and to carry out your monstrous murder!"

"Just now you said it was too bad no one on deck had heard Dida cry out," added Al. "How did you know anyone else was out on deck or that she cried out – unless you were there!"

"Clever – but not clever enough," said Jolyon Scrupulous with a sneer. "In case anyone was smart enough to figure it out, I brought this." He brandished a canister and ran to the door. "And outside my turbo-charged floatamota is waiting. Ha, ha!" the villainous magnate yelled. He pressed a button on the canister. The room began to fill with foul-smelling smoke...

Suddenly, a familiar voice came from just outside the doorway. "Not so fast, buster. Where do you think you're going?"

45

# A Familiar Face

The clouds of trianide gas cleared slowly away. And there, framed in the doorway, stood Dida! She lifted her hand up to her head...

You thought you'd finished me off – but not so!

Then Dida began her tale. "The storm was easing when Jolyon Scrupulous burst into my cabin," she said. "He cried out that JJ was missing and rushed out on deck. I ran after him. Next thing I knew he was dragging me to the rails. I struggled hard but it was no use!"

"I was going down for the third time when something nudged me to the surface," Dida continued. "It was a friendly poropista – and a few feet away the Potted Shrimp was drifting by! I hauled myself aboard. Hours later, I was picked up by a fishing boat."

"I blurted out my story. Immediately, the fisherman chased after the Prancing Prawn. At last we caught up and clambered aboard. The fisherman went below to try and stop the engine. I followed the sound of voices. I got here just in time, it seems." She turned to Al and Dan. "But how did you guess who I was?"

"We noticed your tattoo when you came to your cabin door," said Dan. "We saw a strand of red hair as well, so we knew you were wearing a wig. And the magazine had shown a picture of Jolyon Scrupulous's partner with a tattoo and red hair! Then, later, Max mentioned your impression of the Captain. You used to be Teeny Dimple!" Dida blushed and nodded, then Dan continued. "The Mythagram in Jolyon's cabin clinched it. You had to be his missing partner!"

"Yes," said Dida. "We invented SLIME. It was a runaway success but that wasn't enough for Jolyon. He moved into dodgy business deals. After the Tuffaware take-over I threatened to report him to the fraud squad."

"Jolyon was mad with rage," continued Dida. "It seemed safer to disappear for a while. With the help of the fraud squad, I faked my death. I left my clothes on a lonely beach... But I still needed one last piece of evidence so I got myself this job – "

"I admit it," said a shamefaced Scrupulous. "I saw your tattoo as you picked up your hat when we first arrived. I panicked. Forgive me!"

Dida looked sternly at him, then spoke.

You have a choice. Give your fortune away – or go to prison!

Jolyon Scrupulous looked at Dida in amazement. Everyone waited in silence, wondering how things would turn out...

The crestfallen magnate paced the room.

...my fortune!

...my freedom!

...fed up with being bad.

...a new leaf?

...a chance to change?

Then he spoke.

This will be my newest and greatest challenge – being good!

h, yes! I will live e simple life in ne small cottage! ere will be roses ound the porch. small puppy will urled at my feet! hall bake bread! me your charities can hardly wait!

Everyone called out.

Happy Days Uzzu Haven!

Bully Beaters!

Penniless Parents!

Hrrrmph... Distressed Detectives.

Just one more thing...

What about those two?

Rula had a suggestion.

I shall need more uzzu keepers in the sanctuary!

We always wanted to go straight...

...and work with animals – or children.

Then...

TOOT!

The boat was slowing down. The engine was mended. And this must be Bigalos!

Toot!

Ah, here's my gallant rescuer!

Al and Dan gasped. So *this* was the gallant rescuer! And he had something to say...

Remember, every journey must end, but the tide will always go on turning!

47

# Detective Guide

This page will give you some help in solving the case. The numbers written here refer to the numbers inside the magnifying glasses found throughout the book.

1 Read the letter carefully. You might want to look at it again later.
2 Don't disregard the advice of the mysterious stranger.
3 Some of this information might be very useful.
4 Keep your eyes peeled here.
5 Take a good look at the smiling duo. You may not have seen the last of them.
6 An interesting book title . . . you wouldn't miss that again, would you?
7 If the Captain didn't order the crate, who did? (You won't be able to answer this now.)
8 Rula's luggage could be worth studying closely.
9 This odd discussion may make more sense later.
10 Keep your ears open here.
11 Who could that voice be hissing about?
12 Take your time over this.
13 Keep a close eye on things, particularly the preparations for the banquet.
14 Study all the statements carefully. Not everyone may be telling the truth.
15 Al has lots of questions. Can you answer any of them?
16 Al and Dan can't see as clearly as you can. Keep your eyes peeled.
17 Don't disbelieve Dither – he used to be a night-watchman.
18 Dither is right. What a lot of lucky escapes the potential victims have had.
19 Right again. At the heart of the matter lies motive – and you need a strong one for murder.
20 Can you remember what Dither said when he asked for everyone's statements?
21 Those prototypes are worth a fortune – to all sorts of people. And check out those boxes carefully.
22 Is this an idle boast? Maybe not.
23 Look at the note. Do you recognize anything?
24 At least one thing Mona says is right.
25 There's more to this page than might first appear.
26 A shadowy duo at the window – but who?
27 Could Dither be on to something?
28 The Bunglas could be giving away more information than they realize. Listen hard to their story.
29 Is Dither right? Or is he looking at things the wrong way around?
30 Read everything thoroughly. You might find some interesting new information – and don't forget about the importance of a strong motive.
31 Listen to the conversation of the shocked group at the table. Does this give you any more clues?
32 Would anyone really mistake Dida for Jolyon?

# By the Way . . .

Now you've read the story and solved the mystery, check whether you spotted every clue. If you have difficulty reading this try holding the page in front of a mirror.

Did you spot the Prancing Prawn flying a red and white flag while at anchor on pages 4 and 5, instead of the normal Mythikan flag? This is an old Mythikan naval tradition, and is noted in the tourist brochure on page 7.

The Bunglas both had spotted neckerchiefs on page 9 but Klava's is fell off when they went foraging for provisions (you can see it on the deck on page 11). They stole the melons from the galley and started scoffing as they went back. Klava noticed his neckerchief on the deck and picked it up, but in his rush to hide he left the end sticking out of the crate on page 14.

Did you see the copy of the Beginner's Soothsaying course book in Cliff's cabin on page 11? On page 34 Cliff and Rula had a copy. So that was what they studied at evening class.

Did you recognize Rula from the photo in the Happy Days Hideaway brochure in her luggage on page 12?

On page 13 Mona had a mobile phone – a clue that she was not shouting at Jolyon, but down the phone.

On page 17 she came out of the changing room, again with a phone. This time she was talking to her sister, Nora. (There is a letter to Nora on page 41.)

Did you get all the clues in the magazine pictures? The hand of Jolyon's former partner was resting on the car door frame, with a tattoo showing. Max was in the school photo, wearing a Mythikan badge. And did you spot the Siblant's tail poking out of the tree?

Plenty of people passed the dining room window on page 20. The clock next to it showed when they did so. Did you notice Mona say, "I eat like a bird,"? Even Jolyon wasn't wicked enough to murder his wife. So he swapped plate with the only person he was sure wouldn't eat enough for the poison to work.

Did you recognize the silhouette of Bala Bungla in the engine room? If you were very sharp-eyed you might also have recognized his watch, first seen on page 9.

JJ was reading a book upside-down on page 32. The title should have given you a clue to the villain.

First published in 1993 by Usborne Publishing Ltd, Usborne House, 83-85 Saffron Hill, London EC1N 8RT, England.
Copyright © 1993 Usborne Publishing Ltd.

The name Usborne and the device 🐝 are Trade Marks of Usborne Publishing Ltd.